3/2/71

Rhodes 3-5

HEATHER GOES TO HOLLYWOOD
by Sheri Cooper Sinykin

Illustrations by
Jordi Torres

Spot Illustrations by
Rich Grote

MAGIC ATTIC PRESS

As members of the

MAGIC ATTIC CLUB,

we promise to

be best friends,

share all of our adventures in the attic,

use our imaginations,

have lots of fun together,

and remember—the real magic is in us.

Alison   *Keisha*

Heather   *Megan*

Contents

Chapter 1
Just One More Time
7

Chapter 2
Answers in the Attic
15

Chapter 3
Heather's Calling
23

Chapter 4
Where's Rena?
31

Chapter 5
The First Act
37

Chapter 6
Two Different Stories
45

Chapter 7
Heather Meets Her Public
53

Chapter 8
All That Glitter
63

Heather's Diary Note
69

Chapter

One

JUST ONE
MORE TIME

an't we *please* stop by the video store?" Heather
Hardin begged her friends on the way home
from school.

"Again?" Keisha raised one eyebrow. "What does that
make? Five times this week?"

"Six. Don't forget Sunday," said Alison. "But, hey,
who's counting?"

Heather only shrugged. The more times she entered her
name in the drawing, the greater her chances of winning the

"Spend a Day in Hollywood with Suzi Paris" contest.
Winners from across the country would fly to Los Angeles
to attend the premiere of Suzi's first movie. From what
Heather had already seen of the young actress in her TV
series, Suzi was sure to be a hit on the big screen, too.

Heather could just imagine how thrilling it would be,
getting all dressed up for the movie's first showing and
hanging out with Suzi Paris and the other stars. So many
photographers would be there snapping pictures that
Heather was sure to be in one of them. Maybe she'd even
get discovered! But only, she reminded herself, if she won
the contest.

"Go ahead, Heather," Megan said. "We'll wait."

"Thanks!" Heather grinned. "It'll only take a sec." And
it was true. She could practically fill the form out with her
eyes closed. *Why do you want to win? Because I love everything
about the movies! I can even say the lines to all my favorites by
heart, so I know what I'm talking about. Suzi Paris is going to be
the next great kid star. And I want to be there when it happens.*

There. Done. Heather signed the paper, folded it
in half, and deposited it in the fancy display box on
the counter.

The man at the register cleared his throat. He was
wearing a tuxedo with a pink cummerbund; the women
who worked there wore them, too. "Stuffing the ballot box

again, I see?" He winked at Heather. "Say, they just released an old classic you'd like. Both copies are out already, but one's due back tomorrow morning. Want me to hold it for you?"

Heather nodded eagerly. "Maybe I can get my friends to watch it."

The man waved and Heather hurried back outside to tell Keisha, Alison, and Megan. Her friends weren't much into old black-and-white movies, she knew from past experience, and she felt silly for not even asking the title. But maybe they'd trust the video guy's recommendation. "So, what do you think?" she asked the girls. "It's supposed to be great, a real classic. Want to come over tomorrow and watch it?"

Alison looked at the others and hesitated. "I'd rather go to Ellie's," she said finally.

"Me, too," chimed in Megan. "We haven't been there all together in—forever, it seems like."

Heather pursed her lips to one side. Megan had a point. Even an old classic couldn't compare with going over to Ellie Goodwin's and playing in her attic. Surely they'd find some wild new outfits to try on and then—

well, who knew what new and exciting adventures awaited them once they looked in their neighbor's mirror? Heather still had a hard time believing all the amazing places she'd gone—not to mention all the incredible things she'd done—since she and her friends had formed the Magic Attic Club.

"Maybe we could do both," Keisha suggested gently. "Go to Ellie's and then go to Heather's."

"Tell us again," Alison teased. "What's so great about old movies?"

Heather gave a withering sigh. Where was Ali's imagination, her sense of romance? How could Heather explain stuff like that?

"I'm sorry." Alison flashed that infectious McCann family smile. "It's just that . . . honestly, Heather, you get so into them."

Heather pretended to pout. "Okay, okay. But that's what movies are for."

"I know, but I kind of see what Ali means. These are so . . ." Keisha rolled her eyes, then tossed her hair back for dramatic effect. "Oh, darling," she said, fluttering her eyelashes at Alison, "we are so purrrr-fect together! Promise me we will live happily ever after."

Alison took a dramatic step toward Keisha, placing her right hand firmly over her heart. "Yes, you have my

word of honor as a gentleman.
Happily ever after—as long as you
stay purrrr-fectly thin and beautiful
and do what I say. Promise?"

"I do, darling." Keisha crossed her
eyes at Alison and giggled. "Till
death do us part, I promise. As long
as you make us purrrr-fectly rich."

"Etcetera, etcetera," Megan
chimed in, making her voice sound
as boring as Mr. Peters' in science
lab. "Corny music. Fade to black.
The end."

"That's just not fair," Heather said indignantly.
"They're not *all* like that."

"If you say so." Keisha readjusted her new fanny pack.

"I bet you anything you'd love 'em, too," Heather said,
"if you just gave 'em a chance. Okay?"

Megan clapped an arm around Heather's shoulder.
"Well, of course we'll come. Don't look so worried. All for
one and one for all, right?"

"Right!" Keisha high-fived Megan, then Heather in
turn. "Ali?"

Alison had been bumping her soccer ball off her
knees, first one, then the other. She looked up, startled,

at the sound of her name.

"We told Heather of course we'd watch that movie tomorrow, right?" repeated Megan.

"Oh, sure. Right. We'd do anything for you, Heather," Alison said. "You should know that by now."

Heather bit back a grin. "Well, in that case, how about entering my name in the drawing? Please? Just one more time."

"Heather!" the Magic Attic Club members said all at once. But Heather could see that they, too, were trying hard not to smile.

Chapter
Two

ANSWERS
IN THE ATTIC

 nip, snip, snip. The sound of Ellie Goodwin's pruning shears broke into Heather's thoughts. She had already said good-bye to her friends. But how long had she been standing here, Hollywood daydreaming, on the sidewalk across from her own house? "Hi, Ellie!" She waved. A stubble of dead twigs littered the greening lawn. "Need any help picking those up?"

"Thank you. Maybe later. But I'll tell you what I *could* use right now."

"What's that?"
Heather asked.

"A cup of tea and a
visit with you. It's so
rare we have a chance
to simply sit and talk."

"I know." Heather and
the other Magic Attic Club
girls sometimes felt a bit guilty
running up to their neighbor's attic without first spending
time with Ellie. But their friend was often busy giving
music lessons and always urged them to take the key and
go play. "Want me to put the water on?"

Ellie nodded, and Heather raced inside the old
Victorian house to the kitchen. Monty, Ellie's terrier,
tagged along at her heels. While she waited for the kettle
to sing, she phoned home to tell her mother where she
was. Before long, Ellie joined her and quickly assembled
a tea tray with china cups, silver sugar tongs, and thumb-
print cookies filled with jam.

They settled into the den. The aroma of steaming
licorice curled from the teapot as Ellie poured. "Isn't this
nice?" she asked. "Cream? Sugar? One lump or two?"

"Three!"

Ellie bowed her head ever so slightly and smiled.

"I'll bet it's like this in Hollywood, isn't it?" Heather said dreamily. "Getting what you want, even if it's more than what you really need."

Ellie sipped her tea and raised one eyebrow.

"I mean, why stop at one diamond bracelet when you can have three!" Heather sighed, imagining herself again in the company of all those glamorous movie stars. Maybe Megan, Keisha, and Alison couldn't understand the call of Hollywood, but Ellie Goodwin surely could. A long time ago, she'd gone there herself. "That's how it is, right, Ellie?"

Ellie sidestepped Heather's question with one of her own. "Why this interest in Hollywood? Are you planning on taking a trip?"

"If I get lucky." Heather explained about the drawing at the video store. "Maybe next time you go by there, you could fill out a ticket for me?" Her voice squeaked hopefully.

"Well, I do have a film to return." Ellie winked. "But if you don't mind, I have a suggestion. Perhaps you should make your own luck, instead of waiting for it to happen."

Heather frowned. How could she go to Hollywood without winning the contest? "I don't get what you mean," she admitted at last.

"Oh, you will." Ellie smiled serenely as she set her cup

down. "When we're done talking, why don't you go up to the attic and think about it, dear? And I'll finish my trimming outside."

For all the times Heather had visited Ellie Goodwin's attic, she had never before noticed the stack of old magazines near the open steamer trunk. She wondered whether Ellie had been doing some cleaning or reorganizing. Taking an armful, she sat cross-legged on the oriental carpet and began flipping through them.

Images of film celebrities from the 1940s shone from the pages, along with the likenesses of World War II generals and then-President Franklin D. Roosevelt. One article had a picture of some famous Chinese theater in Hollywood where movie stars were honored by leaving their handprints and footprints outside in the cement sidewalk. Heather wondered whether the place still existed. Would Suzi Paris be asked to put her handprints there, too? In one magazine, she found a review of *Star*

Baby, a new film starring Rena Malone. The reviewer called her the "Sweetheart of the Forties." An accompanying photo showed the young star in a pouty pose for the camera.

Was Hollywood as exciting today as it appeared to be fifty years ago? Ellie seemed to think there was more than one way to find out. Replacing the stack at last, Heather crossed to the wardrobe and began rummaging through the drawers. A pair of long white gloves caught her eye. She tried them on, but they looked pretty silly with her play clothes. Surely in the old steamer trunk she could find something more appropriate to wear.

As she pored through the jumble of outfits, a flash of silver caught her eye. "Wow!" Heather's pulse quickened as she pulled out a long, fitted gown. The glimmering silver fabric, woven with pink, shimmered in the light. The bodice was studded with jewels, and a sequined purse was tied to one of the shoulder straps. "This would be perfect to wear to Suzi Paris's movie premiere!" All I need now is a touch of...what?"

Again, Heather delved into the trunk. Finally, she surfaced with a white feather boa. "Oooh, it's perfect!" she squealed.

She wasted no time in trying on the whole ensemble. Surely Suzi Paris wouldn't be wearing anything more—

more—Heather fumbled for the right word—more *Hollywood* than this!

Delighted at the image of herself dressed to attend the premiere, she twisted her hair into an elegant French twist. Holding it in place with one hand, she approached the mirror.

With some imagination, Heather could almost believe that the "Sweetheart of the Forties" stared back at her. Drawing closer to admire her glamorous reflection, she wondered whether she'd be able to make the same pouty expression that she'd seen in the old movie review photo. Her first attempt made her giggle, but her second wasn't half bad. A little more angle in the chin, she thought. And lower the eyelids just…so.

"You'll have a better chance if you'll just be yourself."

Startled, Heather whirled away from the mirror. Blinking up at her was a round-faced girl with hair the color of a new penny coiled into ringlets. Ellie's attic was gone, and in its place Heather found herself in some kind of waiting room. Its walls, half-paneled and half-mirrored, reflected scores of other girls, all dressed, as Heather was, in stunning gowns. A titter of nervous excitement zipped about like electricity.

A better chance at what? Heather wondered. But all she said was, "Thank you—I think," and smiled at the younger girl, who she hoped might provide a few more clues about where they were. Even after all Heather's experiences through Ellie's attic mirror, she still found the first few minutes of a new adventure a bit unsettling. What, for example, were those printed pages the girls seemed to be reading from?

"Oh. Didn't you get a script?" the girl asked, reading her mind. Heather shook her head. "You probably shouldn't go in there cold. Here, take mine."

"Are you sure?"

The girl nodded. "You'd be doing me a favor. Really."

Before Heather could even ask why, a door opened on the far side of the room. A hush blanketed the gathering of girls.

Chapter
Three

HEATHER'S CALLING

 stern-faced woman stood in the doorway, consulting her clipboard. She motioned sharply to Heather's would-be friend. The girl sighed, rolled her eyes, then dutifully crossed the room.

From the magazines in Ellie's attic, Heather recognized the woman's hairstyle and clothes as being from the 1940s. Still, she couldn't imagine what her job was or why the girl who'd given her the script seemed so dejected—especially when, as soon as the woman and the girl had disappeared, the others bubbled over again with excitement.

Finding a chair, Heather turned her attention to the script. But she couldn't concentrate. Her stomach was full of butterflies. It was as if she had caught them somehow from the other girls.

"Is it your first time, too?" A blond near Heather nervously fingered a long strand of beads. Heather nodded vaguely. "How many of us do you suppose they'll ask back to screen-test?"

Screen-test! Hoping to mask her surprise, Heather merely shrugged. But now her heart was beating double-time. Could she really be at a Hollywood casting call? "I don't know about you," Heather said at last, "but I could use some more practice."

The girl nodded. "That and a lot of luck." Edging away, she turned to primp in front of the mirror.

Heather tried to read all the way through the part of Vanessa, the rising starlet. But she was too awestruck to concentrate and kept staring at the same page. This was even better than going to a movie premiere, she thought in amazement. Imagine, me, Heather Hardin, a star!

After a time, the casting director appeared again in the doorway. She called another girl out to audition. With mixed anticipation and dread, Heather awaited her own turn. When it came at last, she followed the woman into a larger room, where two men were seated behind a table facing Heather.

"Let's see you walk, honey," the woman said, taking a chair alongside the men. She motioned Heather closer. "Head up, shoulders back. That's right. Like you're a star."

Heather tried to ignore the fluttering in her stomach and played along. The two men took turns snapping orders: "Turn side." "Now the other." "Smile. Give us a bit more teeth." "Sit."

"Here?" Heather asked, indicating a canvas director's chair.

"Exactly." The woman rose, and, patting her tight dark bob, came closer as if to inspect a new doll. "Amazing!" She tipped Heather's chin upward, studied her profile for a long moment, then nodded approvingly. "This one bears an uncanny resemblance to . . ." Here she turned to the men and mouthed something that Heather couldn't hear. "Don't you think so, Roy?"

"It's quite remarkable, really," said the man with the

mustache. "It's too bad we're not casting an understudy. We're not, right?"

The woman appeared to be lost in her own thoughts. At first she said nothing. Then she started nodding. "Roy, you're a genius! Are you thinking what I'm thinking? It's absolutely brilliant! Harry? Are you with us? No? Let me spell it out then."

Heather shifted her weight in the chair. She wished she could hear what they were whispering about. Weren't they going to ask her to read something? Surely the audition involved more than just looking at her.

At last the conference broke, and the tall, gray-haired man—the one called Harry—stood and cleared his throat. "Miss Hardin, we'd like to ask you back to do a screen test—you and several other girls. But we have a rather pressing need right now," he said. "An immediate and terribly important assignment, as it were."

Now the other two stood as well, and the entire group approached Heather. "You see," the casting director went on, "one of our studio's biggest stars is—how shall I put this?—unable to accept an award tonight from the Movie Actors' Guild. The Maggy, it's called. And since you bear such a striking resemblance, well, we were hoping that you'd be willing to stand in for her."

"Omigosh!" Heather's hand flew to her mouth. "Me? Accept an—an award? For whom?"

"Rena Malone," Roy said. "Surely you know her work."

"Rena Malone? Oh, yes! Of course. But I...I never thought... never imagined ..." Me, Heather Hardin, standing in for one of the greatest child actors of all time! Heather clamped her mouth shut abruptly, not wanting to sound like some starry-eyed kid. Not when they were expecting her to act like a *real* star. Tonight!

"Then you'll do it?" Roy asked.

"You really think I can?"

"Stick with us, kid." Harry winked down at her. "I might be the producer—and Roy here, he might be the director—but we don't call Jean Maloney the Star Maker for nothing."

The woman's no-nonsense expression softened. A dimple creased one cheek. "What's this Maloney baloney?" She turned to Heather. "Call me Coach Jean. It's an all-purpose title."

"Coach Jean it is!" Heather's grin turned suddenly upside down. "Excuse me, but where is Rena, anyway? Why do you need me to accept her award?"

Coach Jean and the director looked quickly at each other, then away, and it was the producer who finally replied. "Rena is, shall we say, unwell. At this time, she's not up to meeting her public."

"Oh, no. Is she in the hospital? Is she going to be all right?" Heather searched the grown-ups' faces. Their masklike expressions heightened her concern.

Harry, the producer, put his hands on Heather's shoulders. "Let *us* worry about Rena," he said. "That's our job, not yours."

"But what's my—"

"Your job is to buy us—I mean, her—some time, Heather," Harry explained. "If the press believes you're really Rena, they won't be looking anywhere else, trying to dig up dirt. Do you understand?"

"I-I guess so," Heather said, though she didn't really. Still, she didn't want them to think she was dumb.

"Put it this way," Coach Jean said. "With the Maggy Awards being held at Grauman's Chinese Theater, everybody who's anybody will be there tonight. Rena can't afford not to make an appearance."

"Precisely," the director chimed in. "A no-show could cost the studio a pretty penny on *Star Baby* at the box office, too."

Heather's eyes grew wide. Was it really up to her whether Rena's new film would be a hit?

Chapter

Four

WHERE'S RENA?

rust me, gentlemen. This will work out perfectly,"
Coach Jean said over Heather's head. "I'll take her
home with me. Teach her the speech, the walk, the laugh.
Leave it to me. By tonight, she'll not only look like Rena
Malone. She'll be Rena Malone." Grasping Heather's
upper arm, she tried to steer her from the room, but
Heather resisted. "Come along, dear."

"I-I don't…" Heather's voice trailed off. She knew she
should probably be grateful for Coach Jean's help, but the

woman was a total stranger. Besides, her sudden take-charge manner made Heather uneasy. Turning to Roy, she beamed a silent plea in his direction.

"Tell you what," the director said. "You meet Rena's little sister, Sophie, and ask her all about living in Beverly Hills. If you two don't hit it off right away, I'll eat my hat."

"You mean, Rena and Sophie both live at Coach Jean's?" Heather asked.

"Well, of course they do," the producer said.

"She's a sweet kid, that Sophie," Roy added. "Got a lot of heart."

"That's true," Coach Jean said. "I just wish it were in the right place."

"Oh, it will be." The director's mustache followed his smile. "If we could just find her the right script, she'd be bigger than Rena. Mark my words."

Heather tried to remember a child actress from the forties named Sophie.

The producer fumbled in his leather case for a moment, then handed Jean two typewritten sheets. "Rena's acceptance speech," he said.

"Thanks." Coach Jean gave each of the men a quick air kiss. "I'll have Sophie work with her on this. She needs to have it down cold."

"Splendid!" The director turned to Heather, clasping her hands in his. "You won't let us down, now, will you, Miss Hardin? Remember, from here on in, you're Rena Malone."

Coach Jean's quick footsteps echoed down the hall, and Heather hurried to catch up. I'm RE-na. I'm RE-na. I'm RE-na, she recited silently in time to the beat. It was hard to believe that behind these closed doors, moviemakers were shooting scenes, clapping boards together, calling "Quiet on the set! We're rolling!" and "That's a wrap!"

When they reached the carpeted offices labeled ROY IRVING FINE, a receptionist started to say, "Mrs. Maloney, your daughter's —" But Coach Jean bustled past, cutting her off with a wave of her hand.

Heather tried not to gawk at the rich wood-paneled walls, hung with gilt-framed oil paintings. The real Rena, after all, would have been used to Mr. Fine's decor. As she followed Coach Jean into the inner office, she wondered whether they expected her to make Sophie think she was Rena, too.

A ringlet-haired redhead who had been lounging on a chaise sat up with a start. Heather recognized her at once as the younger girl from the casting call. But it was hard to believe that she and Rena were sisters. Unlike the dark and elegant actress, Sophie was fair and soft and round.

One of the girl's freckled cheeks bulged strangely. A thin strand of chocolaty drool escaped her mouth.

"Shame on you, Sophie! No chocolate before mealtime." Coach Jean blustered in like a sudden storm but then apologized. "I'm sorry. I'm only trying to help."

Heather wasn't sure what to think or say. How would Rena act with her sister? Were they close? She settled on a pleasant wave and a simple, "Hi, Sophie."

The girl looked up as if noticing Heather for the first time. Gulping down whatever was in her mouth, she did a double take, then gave a quick smile of recognition. She must remember me from the waiting room, Heather thought.

Coach Jean bridged the awkward moment. "Sophie, this is Heather," she said. "She's going to be Rena's stand-in at the Maggys."

"Oh, really? And what about tomorrow? Is she going to do the handprint ceremony at Grauman's, too?"

Heather's eyes grew wide. This was what she'd read about in those magazines! It was a very big deal. Bigger, probably, than winning a Maggy, since Heather had never even heard of that award before.

"Perhaps." Coach Jean shrugged. "If need be."

"Mother! How could you?" Sophie turned to Heather. "And how could *you* be a part of this? I thought you were trying out for 'Vanessa,' like the rest of us!"

"I-I was, but . . ." Heather couldn't finish. She had been so excited about everything that she hadn't even realized that Coach Jean was Sophie's and Rena's mother.

"Sophie, mind your manners!" Coach Jean glared at

her younger daughter. "Heather's doing this as an assignment from the studio. She's only trying to help."

"That's true," Heather said. "I didn't know—"

"Then *help*," Sophie whispered, and her eyebrows arched deliberately as if she were really trying to tell Heather something else, something more.

Heather, however, could not even guess what that might be.

"Heather's going to come home with us now, Sophie, and I'll thank you to work with her on Rena's acceptance speech," Coach Jean announced in a way that left no room for arguments. She glanced pointedly at the mess of scripts on the floor. "Clean up now, and I'll call for the car."

Sophie knelt to gather up the scripts. Heather joined her. "Did you find something you like?" she asked Sophie. "Roy says you could be bigger than Rena someday. Did you know that?"

"Roy and Mother say a lot of things," Sophie whispered. "But I wouldn't believe them if I were you."

"Why not?"

"Because the truth is—"

"Come along, girls," Coach Jean interrupted. "We don't want to keep our driver waiting, do we?"

Five

THE FIRST ACT

n the back seat of the long, red studio car, Heather pressed her nose against the window. Coach Jean sat between her and Sophie. Probably to keep us from talking, Heather thought. She was dying to know what "truth" Sophie had been about to tell her.

It was strange seeing Hollywood unfurl before her eyes in color instead of in black and white. As the

driver headed for Coach Jean's house in nearby Beverly Hills, Heather snapped photographs in her mind. Her favorite was of vibrant green coconut palms brushing a jewel-blue sky. No smog yet, she thought, remembering the yucky yellow blanket that had spread over Disneyland when she'd gone there with her cousins.

"Wow! These homes are amazing," Heather said.

"Wait till you see ours, dear," Coach Jean smiled. "I think you'll be glad you decided to come."

"I'm sure I will," Heather said politely. She didn't want to admit that her imagination was running wild, trying to picture what Sophie's and Rena's bedrooms would look like. And their closets! Surely they'd be overflowing with fancy dresses and toys and more dolls than a girl could play with in a lifetime. Not that Heather would have time for playing. She still wanted to find out what was wrong with Rena. And there was that Maggy Awards speech to practice, too.

At last the driver pulled into a circular drive in front of a sprawling, Spanish-style mansion. It was set well back from the road on an estate surrounded by a spiked wrought iron fence. Neon-colored flowers spilled from the balconies, while water danced atop a fountain in the center of the turnaround. Large exotic blooms that looked like tropical birds graced the walkway to the front door of the house.

"Sophie," Coach Jean said, "please show Heather to the guest room, will you? And get her a dressing gown."

"Why can't she stay in my room?" Sophie asked.

"That would be fine with me," added Heather.

Coach Jean looked from one girl to the other, then shook her head. "No, I don't think so. You need your privacy, Heather, and Sophie will talk your ear off if you let her."

Sophie rolled her eyes but said nothing. Coach Jean motioned the girls toward the house, while she turned back to tell the driver what time to return to pick them up that evening.

"Come on," said Sophie.

Heather tried not to gape as she hurried through the house after Sophie. It wasn't only the size of the rooms but also the colors and textures of the furnishings that amazed her. Everywhere she looked seemed to spring from the picture-perfect pages of some decorating magazine or guide to the homes of the rich and famous.

The two-story house surrounded a central patio. At the sight of a closed door at the head of the curving staircase, Heather's pulse quickened. Was that Rena's room? Was she there right now? Heather wondered whether she dared ask Sophie to let her go in and see for herself. But when Sophie walked past the door, Heather decided to say nothing. At least not then.

Farther down the hall, Sophie pointed out her own bedroom and finally the guest room where Heather was to stay. It overlooked the patio. A vase of fresh pink peonies brightened the massive dresser and picked up the hues in the woven rug and bedspread.  Exquisite perfume bottles displayed on a mirrored tray decorated the vanity. "Do you like it?" Sophie asked.

Heather nodded eagerly. "Coach Jean is so nice to let me stay here."

"She has her reasons," Sophie muttered. She started to explain, then stopped with a frown when footfalls echoed in the tiled hallway. "Shush," Sophie ordered. "Here she comes. Pull out that speech. Act like we're already rehearsing."

Heather obeyed, not wanting to cause trouble for

either of them. She felt as nervous and unsure as if she were performing her first play. This was live and there would be no dress rehearsal.

"Just convince her you can pass as Rena," Sophie begged. "There will be no living with her otherwise."

"But why?" Heather blurted out. "Surely she can't be that bad."

Sophie sighed. "Right now, she is. She's frantic about Rena. We all are. Mother's just got a strange way of showing it."

Heather began reading aloud in the middle of the speech. Coach Jean poked her head in and nodded approvingly. "Hard at it already," she said. "That's the spirit." She turned to Sophie. "You come get me once she has it down pat. I'll work with her then. And if you girls don't dilly-dally, that should still leave time for a nap before dinner."

"I don't see why you just don't—" Sophie began, only to be cut off by a snap of Coach Jean's fingers.

"That's enough, young lady."

Sophie hung her head. "Yes, ma'am," she mumbled.

"Very well, then." Coach Jean took one last look around the guest room as if to reassure herself that all was in order. "Maria will know where to find me."

Maria, Heather soon learned, was only one of several

servants in the house.

As Heather soaked in steamy, lilac-scented clouds of foam in the bathtub, Rena's acceptance speech, along with Coach Jean's instructions on how to walk and talk and laugh like Rena, raced endlessly through her mind. The thought "Oh please don't let me mess up at the Maggys" came often, too, like a prayer. She only hoped Coach Jean's prediction would come true. "You're a natural," she had assured Heather. "After tonight, we'll make you a star in your own right."

In Heather's excitement over standing in for Rena, she had almost forgotten all about the promised screen test. Still, she knew she had to keep her mind on one thing at a time. And right now, that was on pulling off the greatest acting role of her life. Could she convince the entire Hollywood crowd that she, Heather Hardin, was really the "Sweetheart of the Forties," Miss Rena Malone?

Six

TWO DIFFERENT STORIES

 eather and Sophie sat on either end of a polished dining room table. The dark wood was so shiny that Heather, in her fancy dressing gown and pin curls, could see her own reflection. It sure looked a lot calmer than she felt inside! Noticing that there were only two place settings, she asked, "Aren't your parents going to eat with us?"

Sophie shook her head. "Dad doesn't even live here. They're getting"—here she lowered her voice as if she

were about to say a bad word—"divorced. And Mother—
she's probably still on the phone, working."

One of the servants set a strange, green, thistlelike
thing in front of Heather. "Enjoy your artichoke, Miss
Rena," she said, obviously mistaking her for the star.
"I know it's your favorite."

Heather had no idea what an artichoke was
or how to eat it. Still, she thanked the woman
as she supposed Rena would. Then,
hesitantly, she picked up her knife and fork.
The servant frowned and muttered
something in Spanish.

Sophie giggled. "It's all right,
Pilar," she said. "Rena's just being
silly. You can go now."

As the swinging door to the kitchen flapped closed,
Heather unloosed a sigh of relief. "Thanks, Sophie," she
said. "That was a close one. I didn't realize she'd think I
was Rena."

"It's no wonder that she does," said Sophie. She was
picking the leaves off her artichoke with her fingers.
"Mother doesn't want anyone to know Rena's run away.
Especially not the servants. 'Loose lips sink ships.' That's
what she always says, anyway."

"Rena's what?"

"Oops!" Sophie giggled. "Loose lips. See what I mean?"

"Be serious," Heather whispered across the table. "What do you mean, run away? Your father knows, doesn't he?"

Sophie nodded. With a great sigh, she dipped the ends of the artichoke leaves in melted butter, then pulled them one by one through her tightly clamped teeth. "She's been gone about a day now. Too soon to panic, Mother says. We thought she might be at Dad's but..." Her voice trailed off. "At any rate, he says she's not there." Sophie sounded like she had her doubts.

"But why?" asked Heather. "I'd never run away if I had the perfect life. Fame, money, glamour. Rena's got everything."

"That's what you think! What about friends?" Sophie scowled. "How'd you like it, having a tutor instead of going to school and having a regular life?"

"I-I never thought about it." Heather plucked an artichoke leaf and made a halfhearted attempt to copy the way Sophie was eating it. "But surely it can't be that bad."

"Oh, no? Why do you think I don't try harder to like those scripts Mother's always showing me?" Sophie asked. "I know too much. She can drag me along to the studio, but she can't make me like it."

Though Heather didn't say so, she thought Sophie

was probably just exaggerating. Having a private tutor sounded like fun. And she was certain that a girl like Rena would have more friends than she could count.

Behind Heather, something clattered to the kitchen floor on the other side of the door. Sophie look surprised, and Heather sensed someone standing behind her. She didn't dare look.

"That's really quite unfair, Sophie." Coach Jean sounded either hurt or angry, Heather couldn't tell which. "This envy you have toward Rena has got to stop, do you hear me?"

Sophie's mouth sagged open, but she said nothing.

"Heather, dear"—Coach Jean laid her hand on Heather's shoulder—"you must understand where these crazy stories are coming from. A little sister's overactive imagination—that, and wounded pride. I do what I can to include Sophie. You saw that yourself at the studio. But she has to at least make an effort. A star simply can't sit around eating bonbons, you know."

Out of the corner of her eye, Heather saw Sophie hang her head.

"Surely I told you before that Rena is overworked. She's exhausted, poor dear. She needs a couple of days' rest. Someplace private. That's all."

"But Sophie said—"

"I heard what she said, and that's why I decided to tell you the truth myself, dear. This running-away business, it's absolute rubbish!" Coach Jean glanced at her diamond-studded wristwatch. "Oh, my. You girls had better hurry and finish up here. Ventura will help you dress, of course. But you still have some decisions to make about jewelry, and whether to wear a hat."

"Yes, ma'am." Heather's pulse raced, imagining herself all dressed up for the Maggy Awards. It would be her big moment, her chance to shine and do a favor for the studio at the same time. She was helping Rena, too, by standing in for her, wasn't she? Of course she was. Coach Jean was only doing what was best for both her daughters. And Heather didn't blame Sophie one bit for being envious. She supposed she might feel that way if her own sister, Jenna, were a big star.

Coach Jean came around behind Sophie and appeared to rub her shoulders for a moment. "Now, promise me, Sophie, no more stories, please. Especially not around the press. We need everything to go smoothly tonight, all right?" She kissed Sophie's cheek; then, licking her finger, she attempted to rub away her red lip print. "Heather will do her part. May I count on you to do yours?"

Sophie made a face, but Heather doubted that Coach Jean had seen it.

"Sophia Jean Maloney, do you hear me?"

"Yes," said Sophie simply, which, Heather realized, didn't necessarily answer her mother's question. Coach Jean, however, seemed satisfied and turned to leave.

"Aren't you going to eat?" Heather asked her.

The woman shook her head and smiled. "I can't. Not right now, at least. I'm too nervous," she said. "Besides, I still need to call Mr. Maloney and tell him you'll be standing in for Rena. After all our hard work, that's the last thing we need—her own father's loose lips to go sinking the ship."

At Coach Jean's words, Heather bit down hard on an artichoke leaf to keep from laughing.

"See? What did I tell you?" whispered Sophie, and though she pressed her lips together, Heather saw the giggles building up. Still, that didn't mean everything else Sophie had told her was true as well, did it? If only Heather knew for sure.

C h a p t e r

Seven

HEATHER MEETS HER PUBLIC

s the limo pulled up early that evening in front of Grauman's Chinese Theater, Heather asked Sophie for the fifty-third time, "Are you sure I look all right?"

"You look perfect, *Rena*," Coach Jean cut in, winking at Heather. "See all those photographers? They're waiting for you!"

"For me?" Heather gulped.

The car door swung wide then, and as the driver helped Heather out, flashbulbs exploded like fireworks.

"Miss Malone!" someone called.

"Rena, look here!"

"How do you feel about winning your first Maggy?"

"Rena will be happy to meet with you all after the awards ceremony," Coach Jean announced, taking Heather's elbow and steering her through the crowd.

Sophie tagged behind them. For all the notice the reporters gave her, she may as well have been invisible.

As they crossed the courtyard, Heather glimpsed beneath her feet the cement squares of many famous movie stars. There was Shirley Temple's, signed in 1935. It said LOVE TO YOU ALL. Unlike the grown-ups who had worn shoes, Shirley had gone barefoot to make her prints.

"Your father's holding our seats, dear," Coach Jean said to Sophie as they entered the grand theater. Though she spoke through a smile, it seemed forced and unnatural. "I need to take Rena backstage."

"Are you sure you want to do this?" Sophie asked Heather.

"I want to do what's best for Rena."

"Good girl." Coach Jean nodded approvingly and shooed Sophie along.

"See you later, okay?" Heather waved at Sophie, but the girl's expression was impossible to read. Did she wish Heather luck or not?

As Sophie disappeared down the aisle, Coach Jean's grip tightened on Heather's arm. For a moment, Heather panicked. She felt like a rescuer being pulled under by a drowning person. Could she really convince everyone she was Rena—or was she about to make a total fool of herself, Coach Jean, *and* the studio?

She tried not to gape at all the ornate Chinese decorations in the massive theater. She knew the real Rena wouldn't. Instead, she checked her purse to make sure she had the acceptance speech.

Coach Jean definitely knew her way around the huge hall. "And there's the bathroom you should use, if you need to," she advised Heather, giving her a final once-over. She nodded her approval. "So far, so good. Don't worry now. You'll do fine. And afterward, just look for me. I'll handle everything."

Two quick air kisses later, Coach Jean was gone.

Several other actors and actresses were milling nervously about backstage now. But Heather couldn't let herself gawk or get drawn into a conversation with them.

There were too many ways she might give herself away. Instead, she faded into a far corner, closed her eyes, and waited for her big moment.

"And the winner of this year's Maggy Award for Most Outstanding Young Actress is…" A drum roll rose from the orchestra. "Miss Rena Malone!"

Heather's heart almost leaped from her chest. Still, she forced herself to imitate Rena's slow, measured walk. Though she knew the speech by heart, she clutched the folded paper in her hand for security. Head high. Big smile. More teeth: She could hear Coach Jean's commands inside her head as she crossed the seemingly endless stage to the podium.

A grandfatherly man in a tuxedo awaited her there, the gleaming Maggy statuette in his hands. "Ladies and gentlemen," his voice boomed, "Miss Rena Malone."

Heather's hand trembled as she accepted the award. She tried not to stiffen when the stranger gave her a kiss. Was he frowning? Heather wasn't sure. Hoping to erase any doubts he might have about her, she tossed off Rena's trademark pout. When he smiled in response and gave her a quick wink, Heather's stomach went weak with relief. She approached the microphone. It was almost big enough to hide behind, and she wished she could. Was

the real Rena—wherever she was—listening to this on the radio? The possibility made Heather suddenly self-conscious.

She licked her lips, reminding herself how many people were depending on her. "Members of the Movie Actors' Guild," she began, scanning the first few rows for a glimpse of Sophie, for some sign of encouragement. No such luck. "Thank you so much for this wonderful award." She held the statuette up, as Coach Jean had told her to do. "I can't tell you how much I love what I do, and how much it means to me that…" Heather's voice trailed off. She glanced out at the crowd, gathering in the smiles, the glitter of the gowns and necklaces, the electric anticipation on people's faces. They were excited. They were with her all the way.

How, then, could she explain the hollow, nagging feeling in the pit of her stomach?

"I…um." With shaking hands, Heather unfolded the sweaty paper. As she skimmed the words, she tossed off a little laugh, hoping to set everyone—including herself— at ease. Finally, she found her place. Flushed and breathless, she managed to deliver the remaining lines. But even she could hear how unconvincing she sounded.

When she finished, though, the crowd's approval rolled in waves toward the stage. She supposed that's what really mattered. But strangely, she realized now, she couldn't enjoy it. Not really. Not when it was meant for someone else.

When the applause died a few minutes later, a handsome escort ushered Heather offstage into the wings again. Still clutching the statuette, she glanced about for Coach Jean. But it was Sophie who rushed toward her, a trim, dark-haired man in a tuxedo close behind.

"Rena," Sophie said pointedly, "aren't you going to hug Daddy?"

Heather let the man embrace her warmly. All at once, the smell of his spicy aftershave made her miss her own father, a pilot. She always seemed to be welcoming him home from somewhere. Her eyes felt suddenly hot and she broke away.

"Are you okay?" The man held her at arm's length, his face etched with concern.

Heather nodded quickly. "It's just kind of overwhelming, you know?"

"Tell her, Daddy," Sophie prompted, wiggling in to make an almost group hug.

Mr. Maloney pulled Heather closer and kept his voice

low. "I've received a call about a certain runaway, shall we say. She's with her tutor, Miss Fraser. And I must admit, I am shocked to learn the depth of her unhappiness. I truly had no idea."

"Unhappiness? Really?" Heather blinked up at him as he released her.

Immediately, a pack of reporters engulfed her. Coach Jean, somewhere in the crowd, was trying without success to get everyone's attention.

"It's *your* press conference," Sophie whispered.

"But what am I supposed to say?" Panic made Heather's throat tighten.

"Whatever's best for *you*, Rena," Sophie said pointedly. "I'm sure you'll think of something."

Heather hadn't rehearsed this part, and Coach Jean seemed in no position to be much help.

"Miss Malone, are you excited about tomorrow?" A reporter thrust a huge microphone at her.

"Tomorrow?" Heather's mind went blank.

"The print ceremony," someone reminded her. "Outside. In the forecourt."

"Hey, Rena," another reporter shouted, "are you going to wear shoes or go barefoot?"

"I-I—" Heather glanced at Sophie. The girl's face was so full of hope. "Neither," Heather finally blurted out, to her own—and everyone else's—astonishment. "I won't even be there because…"

Coach Jean was shooting dagger looks at Heather. But they only made her more certain about what really was right. Not for Coach Jean. Not for the studio. But for a girl named Rena who wanted—no, needed—to be heard.

Heather cleared her throat. She found her own voice and Rena's as well. "I won't be there, because I'm not the real Rena, that's why," she said. "I'm a stand-in."

Light bulbs flashed. The reporters all started talking at once. Some pushed more microphones in Heather's face as she extended one hand to Sophie and the other to Mr. Maloney. "Rena, if you're listening, come back home, okay?" Heather pleaded across the airwaves. "We all love you—I mean, your family does. No matter what, they want you to be happy. You have to believe that everything will work out, if you just come home and talk about it."

Chapter

Eight

ALL THAT
GLITTER

he only way Heather could escape the mob of
reporters was to flee to the bathroom. No doubt
Sophie and her mother would be right on her heels.
Heather knew there was no time to lose.

Hurriedly, she pulled a lipstick from her purse and
scrawled a message on the bathroom mirror:

> *Don't worry about me. I've gone back home*
> *where I belong. I hope Rena will, too.*
> Love, H.

At least now, Heather felt sure, Coach Jean would have to listen to Rena—and to Sophie, too. Divorced or not, Mr. Maloney would see to that.

She reread her note, then added, P.S.—*Thanks for letting me borrow these.*

As much as she would have liked to show Ellie and her Magic Attic Club friends her glamorous jewelry, she knew that it had only been on loan. Tucking the necklace and bracelet of sparkling precious jewels inside a handkerchief, she placed them directly beneath the mirror where Sophie and Coach Jean would be sure to see them. Then, with a flip of her feather boa, she blew a kiss to her reflection as Hollywood Heather and said good-bye.

"Ellie!" Heather opened the attic window a bit wider and called again. "Hey, Ellie, up here!"

Ellie, trimming hedges in the backyard, squinted up at her, then cupped a hand to one ear.

Heather, still wearing her Hollywood gown, flapped one end of the boa out the window in the breeze. "I did

what you said! I made my own luck." Though Ellie
nodded, Heather wasn't sure that she had actually heard.
"Just a minute. I'll be right down."

Heather scrambled out of her fancy outfit and into her
play clothes again. Then, grabbing the key to the attic,
she locked the door and hurried downstairs. Monty
yipped to go out with her, so she snapped on his leash
and led him outside.

"Oh, Ellie, you'll never guess where I went!" exclaimed
Heather.

"To the attic, I thought." Ellie winked.

"*Ellie*." Heather pretended to be exasperated. "That's
not what I meant and you know it. I went to Hollywood."

"You don't say."

"I *do*. And I was Rena Malone's stand-in at the Maggy
Awards."

"Well, that's just wonderful,
Heather!" Ellie skimmed her
clippers over the hedge,
making sure it was even.
"Now you'll be all prepared
if you win that drawing,
I guess."

The drawing. Heather
sighed. After what she'd just

seen, she almost wanted to go steal a few of her entry forms out of the box. How could going to Suzi Paris's premiere compare with accepting a Maggy Award? Besides, Heather realized, Hollywood seemed to twinkle brighter from a distance. Kind of like a star.

"Did I say something wrong?" Ellie asked.

Heather shook her head. "You just got me thinking, that's all." She knelt and began gathering up the dead hedge trimmings. "I'm not so sure I want to win anymore."

When Ellie said nothing, Heather pressed on. "Sometimes it's better not to see things too close up, you know? It can spoil the effect."

Ellie gave a sympathetic nod.

Tossing the twigs into Ellie's lawn cart, Heather grew thoughtful again. "I wonder what happened to Rena. Did she ever put her hands and feet in that yucky cement?"

"As I recall, she out-and-out refused," Ellie said. "That square went to—let me see—Esther Williams and some soldier, Heather. And I don't think Rena ever made another movie, either."

"Really? So *Star Baby* was her last one," Heather mused. "I guess I never realized that. Do you think she's still living?"

"I should hope so!" Ellie grinned. "I just saw her last fall at a benefit in Chicago. She's active in a lot of

charities these days."

"Just like you, Ellie!" Heather tried to imagine Rena being fifty or so years older. That would make her and Ellie about the same age.

Ellie fastened the safety latch on her garden shears. "Well," she said, "that's enough of that." Monty, impatient, began to tug at the leash. "Looks like he wants to go for a walk, eh, Heather? Do you want to come along?"

"Sure."

Ellie grinned. "How about we go to the video store? You can wait outside with Monty while I go in."

"But you don't need to—"

"No arguments now. Just let me get my things."

Before Heather could protest, she was holding Monty and Ellie was heading for the house. When she returned a few minutes later, a purse on her arm and a videotape in hand, Ellie glanced at her watch. "Good," she said. "We'll make it before six."

"What happens at six?" asked Heather.

"No more 'early bird bonus bucks'. Remember, Heather, a dollar saved is a dollar earned." When Heather frowned, Ellie explained, "This isn't due until tomorrow, you see, but if I return it early, then they pay me."

"Oh, I get it. Then they can rent it out sooner and make more money, right?"

"Exactly." Ellie gestured with the hand that held the video. "And I'll bet you this one gets rented before I even put it on the counter."

"Really? What is it?" Ellie held the black case so Heather could read the title. Her jaw dropped in amazement. "*Star Baby*! Oh, Ellie," she cried, "don't you dare let them rent it to anyone but me!"

Diary

Dear Diary,

Surprise, surprise. Guess which video the man at the store was going to hold for me? He's right, though. *Star Baby* is one of the greats. Megan, Keisha, and Alison came over, just like they promised, and they all agreed. Even Alison.

Of course, I told them every last detail about how I stood in for Rena Malone at the Maggy Awards. They wished they'd been there to see me in my big role. Too bad I never got a look at any of those pictures the photographers took!

Yesterday the video store had the drawing for the Suzi Paris contest. I'm glad we weren't limited to one entry. This way, I got to spread my luck around. Would you believe that I won *five* consolation prizes? T-shirts with the movie title on them, and guest passes for when it finally comes to town. That makes one for each of us Magic Attic Club girls, with an extra for Ellie, if she wants to come. Or Jenna, if not.

Oh, I almost forgot. I checked out this book at the library about child actors. I never knew that when Shirley Temple grew up, she became an ambassador to two foreign countries, Ghana and Czechoslovakia. Can you imagine that? I guess there's no limit to what you can be or do when you get older.

So, I think Ellie was right. You can't just sit around waiting to get lucky. You have to go out and make your own luck. From what I can tell, Ellie Goodwin's right about most everything! I guess you could say she's the best neighbor any girl could want, and not just because of her attic, either.

Luv,

Heather